Janice Lee

Reconsolidation:
Or, it's the ghosts who will answer you

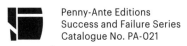
Penny-Ante Editions
Success and Failure Series
Catalogue No. PA-021

엄마,

보고싶어...

I never dreamed about my mother
before her death.

Since her death four months ago, I haven't
been able to escape her in my dreams.

Dreams are closer to the *real* than one thinks,
the logic of this world skewed, falsely multi-
dimensional when really there's only one
dimension that matters, the dimension
we're able to access when the ghosts peel
our eyes closed and remind us of the past
events we so viciously try to tuck away.

A gaping hole I cannot understand:
Is this what trauma feels like?

Memory is a life-long process, wavering between *consolidation* and *reconsolidation*.

Consolidation is the neurological process that stores memories after an experience.

Reconsolidation occurs when a memory is reactivated and therefore destabilized. As previously consolidated memories are recalled, they reenter a vulnerable state and are actively consolidated again. Evidence has shown that the NMDA glutamate receptor – which solidifies memory – is also involved in the memory's destabilization.

Ghosts have no memory, but I do.

The memories congregate like
a slow-moving herd of dots.

[I]f I'm a ghost, but believe I'm speaking with my own voice, it's precisely because I believe it's my own voice that I allow it to be taken over by another's voice. Not just any other voice, but that of my own ghosts. So ghosts do exist. And it's the ghosts who will answer you. Perhaps they already have.

Jacques Derrida

My mother haunts my dreams. Last night I dreamed that she insisted on being there with us, my brother and dad and I, and even mentioned that we should all go out for dinner tonight. *We never eat together anymore*, she insisted. In my dream I told my brother that it hurt, her own denial that she was dead, her insistence on being in our lives the way she used to, but these are my dreams and not hers, so who is the ghost here?

This all becomes a languid conversation, a merging of that space and this one, an atmosphere that is all once too familiar and impossible to make out. As certain memories are destabilized, the way I remember an identity changes, like looking through a hole in the wall from a particular angle, moving away and coming back, looking through the opening again and seeing something else, something different, but all too familiar as it has already seeped into your brain.

Each voyage is a matter of timing, and when things are intended, they slip and fall away. Sometimes it is a strange trigger, her black scarf, tucked on the left corner of my dresser, partially covered from view by a pile of clothes. I can smell the scarf, and hope it still smells like her, a possession once held by her and now held by me but I don't hold it, I leave it there in some presumable fashion. She wore the scarf often on walks, but recently she hadn't been going on them. Honestly, I'm not sure if I remember what she smells like. Everything I've brought back, her things, their smells are all permeated with my father's cigarette smoke.

False memory is a normal phenomenon.

Reconsolidation suggests that when you use a memory, the one you had originally is no longer valid or maybe no longer accessible. If you take it to the extreme, your memory is only as good as your last memory...
The more you use it the more you change it.

Joseph LeDoux

Memories consolidated and reconsolidated
so many times, I don't remember the faces of
my mother anymore. I can see a face, but the
emotional state I'm in, it could really be any
face, every face looks like *her* face. Only dream-
glimpses allow me to see her, but even in my
dreams there are obstacles. In one dream I saw
her, but my brother held me back. *It's Omma,*
I told him. *She's not real. She's dead, remember?
Don't touch her. That's not her.* He grabbed my
hand, led me up a stairway that went nowhere.
We were running away from something, an
incoming fire perhaps. This house is always
on the brink of burning down.

When I saw Eugene last weekend, we talked
about our dreams. He admitted too, that he
had rarely dreamt about her before her death.
But now, she plagued him, in everyday scenarios,
dreams of eating dinner, taking walks, cooking
dinner. He also remembered her death,
the moment it must have happened.

After a traumatic event, some experience a disorder of memory, the event forging a potent and interruptive memory that erupts into view over and over again. The memory becomes relentless, and the more you wish to forget, the more it shows itself, and the less you hear from it, the more you are afraid that you will lose the memory forever.

My mother died of a brain aneurysm.
Her dead certificate states:

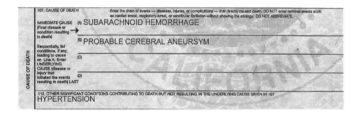

When I reread the words, what I notice is the misspelling of *ANEURSYM*.

I don't remember what time it was when I heard my phone ring. It was late, perhaps around 3 or 4 in the morning. I didn't recognize the number and so I didn't answer. A few seconds later, Jeff's phone started ringing too. It was the same number. He didn't pick up either, but I sensed something was wrong.

The next time my phone rang I picked it up right away. A man's voice asked for Janice. *This is she*, I responded. *Ok, let me put you on with your brother.*

14

During reconsolidation, new information is often incorporated into the old memory. The emotional or psychological state you are in when you recall that memory will inevitably influence the reconsolidated memory. Recalling a memory during these stages of inadequacy, repentance, sought-after impossibilities, recalling a memory under these conditions may be dangerous. The memory, a symbol for a strange form of affliction and permanence of love, may be changed forever.

Replenish this and I will give you that. The entire
neighborhood will. *Dust to dust.* I'm compelled
to remember things over and over again, even
if that's not the way they happened, that's what
I see. It's come to the point, here on the brink
of a mind, the mind ravenous like a shark,
it's come to that point where I only trust what
I see in my dreams.

Janice, I think you have to come home right now.

What? Wait, what happened?

It's Omma. She passed away...

What?! What happened?!

She just collapsed. We're at the hospital right now.
The doctors say her brain is dead.

What?

She's hooked up to a respirator.
We're waiting for you.

Ok.

...

...

...

Ok. I'm coming. I'm leaving right now.

Ok. I won't have reception. I can't leave my phone on in the emergency room. Ask for us at the front desk. She's at San Joaquin General Hospital.

Ok. I'm leaving.

Ok.

It was late. My brother was asleep already and my father was in the other room, finishing up paperwork. My mother was trying to fall asleep but couldn't. She complained to my father about her head. *My head, it hurts.* My father was only a little worried as this wasn't uncommon. She had had migraines, headaches, and dizziness on and off for the last few months due to her high blood pressure. He told her to try and sleep. But she couldn't. Her head hurt too much. *My head, it feels like it's about to explode!* My father was now concerned, so he woke up my brother Eugene. He got up, went to the phone. My mother was screaming in pain. He dialed 911. My father was helping her put on her pants. And suddenly, amidst her screams, she collapsed.

That's when it happened, Eugene told me. *I remember. I just remember that moment, over and over again.*

He had trouble sleeping the first few nights because he couldn't stop remembering.

Sometimes we become frozen in anticipation, wondering what the truth behind a moment is, a life, haunted by the memories littered in the spaces we force ourselves into. Dean Koontz writes, "We are haunted, and regardless of the architecture with which we surround ourselves, our ghosts stay with us until we ourselves are ghosts." But we haunt ourselves, it comes from within, shame and the guilt become the inutterable words, whispered by the wind in passing but unable to pass through our own lips. The impressions left on us become horrific, a face, a stare, closed eyes, and the inert presence of a mother who suddenly is a rare sight, dusty and far, multiple perspectives on a life fall back and a new sequence of events is created, one constituted by the good times, the good times, there were so many moments, pristine and peaceful, but why when she was alive, did I never notice, and why, when she was alive, did I only remember the times we fought, wanted to kill each other, stared at each other with so much hatred, mother and daughter locked in death match after death match.

When the paramedics arrived, they lied and told my brother and father that she would be all right when she got to the hospital. They believed this, so when they arrived at the hospital were not expecting the news:

She's not going to make it.

What?

She had an aneurysm. I'm so sorry.
There's a 0% chance of recovery.

What?

She's dead. There's nothing we can do.

My brother and father didn't sleep that night. When I arrived at the hospital, my brother met me in front of the emergency room desk. He brought me to her. She was lying down, hooked up to a respirator. She didn't look relaxed at all, and though I know she probably couldn't feel anything, she looked miserable, uncomfortable.

She's not breathing on her own.

I hugged my dad. It was the first time
I had hugged him in years.

And then I stood by her bed awkwardly.

You can touch her you know.

I put my hand on her arm.

Feel in her hand, it's still a little warm.

I put my hand on her fist. It was warm inside, but I couldn't pry the fingers open more than a couple centimeters.

One of my most terrifying memories of my mother is when she tried to kill me. Upset over something, I can't remember what, she chased me up to my room, picked up a large, metal paper cutter, and threw it at my head. If I had not ducked, it would have split my head open. It hit the wall behind me, breaking into several pieces. Instead of apologizing, my mother yelled at me for breaking the paper cutter. *Look at what you did!* she screamed. A few months ago, my mother and I were reminiscing about things from before. How Eugene and I used to cheat in our math workbooks and look at the answers in the back of the book. We were caught of course, and what I learned was how to cheat realistically, to purposely get a few wrong to make it more believable. *That was how you taught me how to cheat*, I told her. She was amused. Then I asked her if she remembered the paper cutter incident, how she had almost killed me. She didn't. She didn't remember it at all.

It is when words fail that ghosts appear. It is when memory has something to say, that the ghosts are visible. It's when you touch an object, one that had no significance whatsoever, until its owner died, that you feel you ought to feel something *more*. It's as if you feel like you could gather up some of that person's essence through the objects that they touched, the places they inhabited. It's as if you're looking for the ghosts, wanting them to show themselves, because at least then you wouldn't be alone.

It's as if I can't possibly imagine the future anymore, even though she never pictured prominently in my future anyways. But suddenly, she does, her absence does, and a pile of subjective dispositions to the past, the past becomes changed more and more by the future of her absence.

It becomes unbearable. And I feel more and more alone. We are not a communicative family. Eugene and I don't really talk about our pain. We dwell and analyze the pain of our father, what we should do, how we should proceed, but never about our own pain. But there are those points when it becomes so heavy. When I'm stuck in traffic or on long drives, or waiting, I call my mother. When I was driving back from Pomona one night, I had the urge to call her, but realized right away I couldn't. I could never call her again. It was such an inconsequential realization, that I couldn't call her, not momentous, but heavy. I fought my tears all the way home.

It's because you're Korean, says my friend Dante. *You're strong. You guys are like rocks.*

Though this should be comforting,
it's actually slightly upsetting.

This whole situation makes me feel weak, when the weight becomes too much, when it's morning and *I remember* what's happened and just want to go back to bed. But at the same time, I don't show it. I feel like I'm mostly okay, I'm going to be productive, go back to normal life, and then feel distant, guilty for not being sadder. *I should be more messed up, shouldn't I? I have a good reason to just lie in bed and be sad, don't I? So why do I insist on fighting past it all?*

We were all gathered around her when it was time to unplug the respirator. My dad, Eugene, me. Two families – old friends of my parents, who had driven from San Francisco and Reno – were there too. My aunt and my uncle. Jeff was graciously outside in the parking lot with our dog Benny.

I remember when they unplugged the respirator and all the mucus that spilled out of her nose and throat. My dad's friend asked the nurse to please clean it up. My father and brother and I, we were all silent. I was so self-conscious in those moments. I wanted to be more focused on *her*. I would never see her again, and though she was dead already, I felt like I had to get in as much looking at her face as possible. But what figured more prominently in my mind was that everyone was looking at us. It was the family that was on display, how we were taking it, whether we were crying, how we were dealing with the situation, their pity and sympathy pouring out of their eye sockets.

I remember watching the monitor, her breaths now coming less and less frequently. It would only take a few minutes, they said. But it felt like an eternity. The nurse commented, *She has a really strong heart. That's why it's taking so long. That's why it's still beating. Her heart is so strong.* I was angry. What good was her strong heart doing now?

I remember when she finally flat-lined. In that moment, I felt a tinge of relief, but also a tinge of *Oh-shit-she's-really-dead*. Even though she had been brain dead for all those hours, it hadn't really felt like she was gone yet, like she had just been sleeping there in bed, that she still might wake up.

I remember when we all heard the beep, and when the nurse officially pronounced her dead and jotted down the time of death, that my dad had what is called a psychogenic non-epileptic seizure, collapsed on the ground, started kicking and smashing his head on the floor. Eugene got down on his knees and held my father's head while I grabbed his arms, tried to caress him and calm him down. It took several nurses to keep him pinned, and the entire time he was flailing all his limbs, he kept screaming in Korean, *No, take me instead. You fuckers. You fucking bastards, take me instead. Bring her back and take me instead. Fucking bastards, you're taking the wrong one. Take me. Take me. It's my fault so take me.*

My aunt and I were sent down with my dad on a stretcher to the emergency room. When he snapped out of whatever state he had been in, he asked me what I was doing here. *Why am I in the hospital? Did something happen? Why aren't you in LA?* I didn't want to say the words, so just asked him, *You don't remember?* He stared blankly. The nurse came and went, and then he snapped out of whatever other state he had just been in. *I remember now,* he said. He was weeping softly. *I remember.* He wanted to go back upstairs, say goodbye. I didn't argue, though my aunt tried to. My dad was stubborn and there wasn't really any use.

What I remember is that when we arrived, one of my mom's friends handed me a bag. *Your mother's purse.* I glanced down and recognized it. As everyone slowly shuffled out through the double doors, I lingered behind. I had been sent down to ER so quickly I hadn't had a chance to really say goodbye. I wanted to see her face again. I stood by the bed for a moment, whispered goodbye and maybe some other things that I don't remember right now. But I remember her face. Her face had already turned a light shade of yellow, darkness starting to permeate around her eyes.

I had trouble sleeping the first few nights because I couldn't get that face out of my mind.

I confess that I avoid thinking about my mother. But when a memory breaks away and crosses the threshold of my own constitution, I welcome it, and the tears that follow.

Every time I remember my mother, I transform her with my desire to remember her.

This text becomes a repository of certain
memories, all of which will be changed
or recreated by the end. The memories,
and consequently the text, becomes subject
to continual adjustment and modification.
Simultaneously, the ghosts shift, ask new
questions, recollect their own memories,
and when a passerby knocks at the door
I open it with a welcoming attitude. In my
dreams I catch myself spying on myself,
I become the ghost haunting myself,
as I wander through dream-worlds,
unraveling threads and unable to really
touch anything, but I follow and watch
and see what the memories do to my body,
what they do to me.

*Memory is owed and repaid although
the indebtness is never fully discharged
but continually inherited.*

David Appebaum

When memory is not in question,
neither is identity.

Michael Lambek and Paul Antze

It's as if every action is so meaningless, but
also rife with significance, like I can hardly
succeed in my own way anymore, I have to have
everything justified according to the ghost's
satisfaction. The ghost is the only consolation
that I knew who my mother was at all, that as
time passes I can still have something preserved,
though I know it is more complicated than that.
"Aren't we compelled to remember things over
and over again?" Arkadii Dragomoshchenko
writes. I compel myself to remember so that the
ghost doesn't leave, but I'm usually afraid and
don't allow the memories to emerge from their
proper hiding places. *Was* becomes an awkward
verb, and then suddenly a pristine moment
pops up, keeps me intact for that much longer,
the ongoing recollections that pile up and try
to form some sort of body. Though I realize it's
my own body I'm trying to reconstruct here, not
my mother's, as if because of her death, I'm not
sure who I really am anymore. Every action feels
artificial, and I'm aware of it all as an outsider,
like in my dreams when I can float above my
body, *is that what the soul is?* It's the collection
of memories that constitute my own self that
I can't seem to get a grip on.

My mother was cremated and her ashes spread in San Francisco Bay. My father, racked with guilt, didn't want to board the boat. She wouldn't want me there, he thought. He had taken her away from her family and brought her to America to be poor, to be married to a failure, and it was his fault, he thought. Her children should be the ones to send her off, he thought.

The morning of the service I woke up from a strange dream. I dreamed that we were all camping by the Sacramento River, the way we used to when I was little. My mom, dad, and brother were all there, and all of our family friends. We were eating, playing in the water, laughing. Suddenly the scenery changed and we were on a boat, including my dad. Then, my dad went missing. *Where did Appa go?* my mother asked.

When I told my dad the dream, he thought,
I guess I have to go on the boat. Mr. Lee, a friend
of the family, was driving us. *You have to go.*
Janice dreamed it, it's a sign. So my dad boarded
the boat. I think he was glad he did, that he was
able to use my dream as an excuse to properly
say goodbye to his wife.

40. PLACE OF FINAL DISPOSITION AT SEA OFF THE COAST OF MARIN COUNTY

We're just seeing what we saw before.

*Ghosts and writers meet in their concern
for the past – their own and of those
who were once dear to them.*

W.G. Sebald

It is not hard to imagine a ghost successfully.
What is hard is to imagine successfully an object,
any object, that does not look like a ghost.

Elaine Scarry

I never dreamed about my mother
before her death.

Yet she has haunted my writing all my life.
In all my texts there has always been a mother,
different sorts of mothers, different images
of a real mother sowing the swift canvas
of strange familial bonds.

There is a thin film of muteness over everything
I now encounter, "ghost" just another word
for "mother," just another word for "memory,"
just another word for "gone."

Self-diagnosis is like an attempt to archive something that never was, to grasp the signs of something that evaporates immediately and is only preceded by vague notions of intention.

My mother, a year before her death, was diagnosed with extremely high blood pressure. After she vomited multiple times and then fainted, she was taken to the emergency room. She remained dizzy and nauseous for months afterwards, with a semi-permanent migraine that only dwindled on good days. She started to get much better, back to normal almost, though it was at that point of positivity that, in the early morning of September 5th, 2010, she had a brain aneurysm and was consequently declared brain-dead.

Throughout my mother's struggle with her high blood pressure, which sprouted mostly from her high stress levels, something she couldn't control, I became increasingly observant of my own stress. My mother is a high-stress person. She always has been. She worries about details, is extremely self-conscious, and has trouble sleeping at night. I inherited this from her.

And so did my brother. My brother deals with his stress in different ways. Either ignoring it, not dealing with it all, or more commonly, it comes out in anger. Lately he's been building things, and I think that helps a lot. I've always been high strung too and in recent years, have learned to control it. Basically, the most important thing I learned was to just not care. Sometimes, I don't need to care. Caring causes worrying and worrying doesn't fix anything, so I've tried to adapt a more distant, less-invested state of being. Though this also has helped me to say no, to be more honest, and to be more in control, I realize it's also leaked into other sectors of my life. I am less emotional, which also means I'm less sentimental and romantic, and consequently less affectionate. Probably, Jeff has experienced that more than anyone.

Ghosts wander in and out, but there is only
one ghost I am concerned with. She is a ghost
that comes only when called, and she is rarely
summoned. Who am I, to the ghost, I who
am living? What can someone like me be to a
ghost, but another ghost myself? Do my ghostly
qualities show in public? Do I haunt the spaces
I occupy too? How does the architecture change,
the construction of identity, the strategy for
life when ghosthood is so often self-imposed,
when ghosts are haunted by the ghosts of others,
when I can't rely on my memory of anything
except for the events that occur in dreams.
I'm inclined to continue wandering this complex
labyrinth, the ceiling is low enough to touch
and I can sense the limits of my body, but
something keeps dragging my soul outward,
so I'm constantly struggling with this process
of continual conjuration, a stubborn and
slippery gesture.

Memory is the sense of loss,
and loss pulls us after it.

Marilynne Robinson

Some at least of those left amongst
the living will not escape the excessive
accumulation of memory.

Janet Carsten

I remember dreaming of being in the kitchen, stew bubbling over on the stove, my mother wearing an apron – though she didn't own one – cutting vegetables. We had friends over, they were sitting on the floor playing a game. And it all seemed so normal, so familiar. Inside the dream I had no memory of the real world, but had a slight sense of being in a house I didn't recognize. It was only when I was about to wake up that I remembered she was dead.

It's strange, the disconnect in memory when I am dreaming and when I am not. They say that sleep makes memories stronger, that it reorganizes and restructures them, that naps can help speed up memory consolidation. This may be true. Whenever I wake up I'm always shaken with the intense memory of my mother's my death, the realization that she really isn't alive anymore, though in my dreams I can proceed calmly in slightly familiar scenes, scenes not of comfort or love, but of the mediocre and everyday.

I notice that when I don't think about her, I feel better, life is easier, I feel like I can think about the future. But once I get too comfortable, too settled back into a life that was a different life before this one, I start to feel guilty, as if perhaps I ought to feel more obligated to cart this sadness around with me everywhere, to carry it on my shoulders, spell out the words in distinct murmurs. But I don't. And then, when I do tell people, they always seem so surprised, and I can never quite figure out why. Do I not look sad enough? Should I be more obviously recovering from a mother's death? And then, even worse, they'll say something like, "I'm so sorry about your loss." How does one respond to such a phrase?

I noticed in this strange period of "mourning" (I put mourning inside quotes because I'm not sure what mourning ought to be, and during this period I kept questioning if I was doing it right, if I was mourning properly, if she could see me and she was disappointed that I was being weak, or not weak enough), that my stress levels had significantly dropped, but that my OCD tendencies had shown themselves more visibly.

Of course I took several online tests, and though they are not official tests that can give firm diagnoses, it's always nice to have some kind of validation in writing. Though many of the symptoms or questions were expected, there were also some things I was surprised to see. Of the many questions I was asked to answer yes or no to, I answered yes to a great deal of them.

A few of the questions included:

Have you been bothered by unpleasant thoughts or images that repeatedly enter your mind, such as overconcern with keeping objects (clothing, groceries, tools) in perfect order or arranged exactly?
— Yes. I become physically upset if certain things aren't arranged the way they ought to be. And this is not to say that everything is in alphabetical order or color coordinated. Many of my systems are only systematic in my head, and appear outwardly haphazard, or even a little messy, but I am very certain with the arrangement system. This is most present with my books. I have a very certain system of organization for my bookshelves, and when there are guests, I try very hard to control the urge to watch their every movement as they pull books off the shelf and put them back, though when they are put back they are in the wrong place, or are no longer lined up with all the other books on the shelf. Often times I will remain agitated until I can return things to their proper order.

Have you been bothered by unpleasant thoughts
or images that repeatedly enter your mind,
such as images of death or other horrible events?
— Yes. Especially loved ones. I'll have images
of my dog Benny having died some horribly
violent death, and then I can't get the image
out of my head. And then I fear that I've jinxed
myself, that by having imagined something
so horrible, it now is going to happen, and
then of course the image becomes even more
cemented in my mind.

Have you worried about acting on an unwanted
and senseless urge or impulse, such as physically
harming a loved one, pushing a stranger in front
of a bus, steering your car into oncoming traffic;
inappropriate sexual contact; or poisoning
dinner guests?
— Yes...

Have you felt driven to perform certain acts over and over again, such as checking light switches, water faucets, the stove, door locks, or emergency brake?

— Yes. For example, I for some reason obsessively check to see if my headlights are on or off while I drive. I'll repeatedly flick my finger over the lever to make sure it's in the right position. Sometimes, like when it's raining, I'll do this every few seconds when I become agitated at the thought that my lights might not be on, and then feel utter relief as my finger runs over the notch. On a different note, I'm also very strange about my windshield wipers. The choices for the speed at which the windshield wipers run are utterly inadequate. The first speed is always way too slow, and the the next one up is way too fast. So I will usually manually run my windshielf wipers when I deem appropriate. This will often drive passengers crazy as it seems inefficient and energy-wasting, but I assure you, it's not.

Have you felt driven to perform certain acts over and over again, such as unnecessary re-reading or re-writing; re-opening envelopes before they are mailed?

— Yes. Though I care much less now, and let many more things slide. I used to care more and be much more of a perfectionist. I've trained myself not to care. In high school, I would recopy all my notes neatly in tiny, tiny writing to ensure that I had a clean and neat copy of all my notes. They were impeccable. If I made a small mistake, I would use the eraser. If it was a larger mistake, I would rip out the page and start all over.

Do you recognize that your thoughts or actions are excessive or unreasonable but still feel unable to stop engaging in them?

— Yes.

I wonder about the connection between OCD and memory, the way that these tendencies stem from my memory of my mother, the way that my ability to imagine and be terrified by the future stems from my ability to hold certain images so solidly in my mind, the way these compulsions erupt like memories bursting forth and trying to take control, the ghosts playing tricks on us perhaps, or trying to speak in our place.

Conversations like this are increasingly strange.

— *So do you live in Los Angeles?*
— Yes.
— *Are your parents local too?*
— My dad lives up in Stockton but
my mom passed away last September.

Losing a parent is not the same as losing
a grandparent is not the same as losing a dog.

There are many things I cannot remember.
It becomes increasingly more difficult to recall
her face.

What do you remember?

I remember her eating corn on the cob.
Eating corn reminds me of her.

What else?

I can remember her smell.

The shape of her face?

With some help, yes. But I'm afraid one day
I won't be able to remember her face at all. Or
even worse, the face I remember won't be hers.

Here's what makes me cry: me in the shower,
the landscape substituted by the sound of Benny
barking at the mailman outside. I think, *did
I close the window?* Because I love my dog and
am paranoid that he might fall out the second
story window in his excitement at the mailman
walking by outside. I think, *I really love my
dog and can't wait to get out of the shower
so I can hug him and rub his belly.* I think,
my mom really loved Benny too, loved him
like a grandson, made his favorite foods when
we visited, taped up photos of him all over
the house, sang songs to him. I remember,
the morning after her death, Benny running
around the house, back and forth down the
hallway, sticking his head into each room,
then going back to do it again, sniffing in the
corners, sniffing the carpet trying to track a
scent, looking for someone, looking for her.
This tears me apart, that though memories
are often interpretations, fabrications, they
also reveal the bonds that tie living creatures
together, the bonds that get accustomed to
certain shades of light, certain backgrounds,
and the truth behind the truths of everyday,
the suggestions of what love might be without

language, without the haunting concoctions
of langauge, without the word love, without
the words that describe it, what it might be,
between one and another.

I think, I've been afraid to write lately.
I've been putting it off. Reading, playing sudoku,
rubbing Benny's belly, doing all these other
things instead.

Writing can sometimes be an emotional
experience.

It makes me think, and I haven't wanted
to think too hard about things lately.

I tell myself, and suffer for it:
she will never again be here to see it,
or for me to describe it for her.

Roland Barthes

I think about walking in the park
with Benny and my mother.

Is all mourning so similar?

I want so much for mine to be unique.

My mom is the only family member
I have ever said "I love you" to.

*Psychoanalysis has taught that the dead –
a dead parent, for example – can be more
alive for us, more powerful, more scary,
than the living. It is the question of ghosts.*

Jacques Derrida

My mother had a jade plant on the balcony
that she took care of and cultivated everyday.
She told my dad, *I'm going to keep growing it unto
it produces a flower. That's when I can stop, when
a flower appears.* The jade plant is a special plant
in many Asian cultures. It it rare for the plant
to flower in domestic places, but if it does, it
is considered a sign of good luck and fortune.
My aunt had one in her home too, one she
grew for years without every bearing a flower.

While visiting my father a few weeks ago,
he mentioned that a flower had just appeared
on the plant, that it had just appeared overnight.

I wonder how scorched my face can really get before prayer loses its steam and the moon its air. I stare into the sun too long, the sunsposts, like spirits, invade my consciousness and allow me to believe in another realm that can never truly exist for me outside the memories and dreams of ulterior motives, familiar stirrings, a pillow over my face.

Ghosts do not become angels. That is what the whispers tell me.

In the margins of understanding, I imagine a realm with a beginning and end, with the slowness of a turning head and the speed of a blinking eye. It seems that ghosts reveal themselves as an eye opens, or as a child fills in the colors of a predetermined outline.

The real trouble with angels is that they are not psychic.

Neither is God. Just because he lives inside your brain doesn't mean he can read its secrets.

But at times the sense of having a scrambled memory, of its unpredictable and unreliable performance, makes me feel eroded. Or perhaps the most accurate word is haunted.

Floyd Skloot

There's a sense of haunting that materializes all
the more I try to write this. As if entering the
spaces of words, of images I can't recall so vividly,
as if I fade away in the backgrounds of memories
that show themselves only out of the corner of
my eye. It's difficult to articulate an enounter with
such an event, I mean the reaching out to touch
the dust of dust gone, dust in the wind, dust, dust,
everything returns to dust. A strange ritual I put
myself through, this thing called writing, this
thing called mourning, this thing called remem-
bering. I remember my mother, but not clearly.
I look to a single Polaroid I have of my family,
one of the few photos of our family all together,
my father always the documentarian of the
other three. The Polaroid is many years old.
I look maybe six or seven, my mother's face looks
young, so very different from the face I remember
seeing in the hospital, when I said goodbye to
a corpse, a corpse that once contained the soul
of my mother, but what is a soul without a body,
what does it mean for a body to still have warmth
but be broken, to be dead but recognizable as
somebody once alive. What does it mean to
look at my mother in a photograph, this is what
she looked like, always in past tense, what does

she look like now, scattered ashes in the water, ashes in an urn above my father's bed, a ghost. Sometimes she is a space, the site where her memory is embodied, a sense of her persisting identity, the space around my dog, the furniture in her house. Is this why my father rearranges the furniture every few weeks? Is this why he avoids being home alone for long instances, why he clings to shadows, strange rituals to overcome the repositories of the past while preserving others, anchors of an aura that persists all the more that our own bodies move forward in time.

I feel sometimes that time is moving in the wrong direction. Bodies should move together, how does the past persist in the present and swallow the future? I often think of death now, but never my own, I tell others that I am afraid I will die the way my mother died, but in reality, I'm no longer afraid of dying at all.

What does my father think of
before he closes his eyes as night?

What does my brother see
when he lies in bed trying to sleep?

When will I be able to remember my mother
clearly? Even in my dreams she is blurry, a
shadow, only a *feeling* lets me know it is her.

All the memories are fading away, the familiar transforming into the strange. I am haunted by everything that is disappearing, haunted by what is in front of me, each and every object a link to an absence to a presence to a space inside my head, between the letters there are gaps. The haunting is happening to me inside the gaps. I need the ghosts to stay because without them I may no longer be able to remember, to feel the presence of a certain consciousness, the warmth of a hug that I once tried to shrug off, embarrassed, and now would give up dreaming to feel again. *Give me a kiss before you go. / Do I have to?* Why do we hesitate so much to show affection? In real life and flesh, why do we make things so difficult? I feel as if it's all diverging, my mind is breaking down, my memory is going, not only of her, but *all* of my memories are fading, *all* of my memories are broken, I am broken, this is way too fucking melodramatic, I'm just stalling now, trying to hold on to the integrity of her face, *God, what did she look like?*

It happened to *me*. This is how mourning is a egocentric process. Her death happened to *me*. My memory loss moves through my body like a ghost, the memories that reappear swing my limbs in alternating motions, I am a rearranged body, and again I am stalling. I am stalling.

I never got to properly say
goodbye to my mother.

All I have left is the insistence of her ghost
so that I can have the comfort of her knowing
how I feel *now*.

It's important that she knows how I feel *now*.

Because I can't say goodbye.

It happened to me.

I can't properly end anything that begins
with a death. That isn't the point.

Throughout all this, I realize the limits
of my own knowledge.

I mean, I don't know where she is now.
Nowhere, everywhere, here, there, gone.

I don't know if she could hear me.
I don't know if she can hear me now.

I don't know what her face looks like
without looking at a photograph.

But I do know that there is night and day.
I know that nights are no more difficult
than days, the absence or presence of light
has no effect on memory.

I know that at night I can see the stars, though
most nights the dust shields the luminous balls
and all I can really make out are the lights from
the surrounding city.

I don't know what love is, and may never be able
to explain the silliness of such a word, a four-
letter word meant to encompass way too much.

But I do know that whatever happens between
a mother and daughter in life, cannot stop the
tears from coming at inconvenient moments
in the afterlife.

I don't know what the afterlife is like for others,
but for me, it is the period after a life, after
the life of that woman who brought me into
this world.

I don't know if she was happy for most of her
life, but I do know that when she saw Benny,
she would smile.

I don't know what "death" really means, with all
my stupid and complicated and overintellectual
metaphysical ideas, but I do know that things
have changed.

And I don't know for certain if ghosts exist, but this, all this that I'm living in now, all the words I put together for the sake of some kind of closure, is a site for conjuration, a site of permanent conjuration, because I will be conjuring ghosts for the rest of my life.

Whether I believe in ghosts or not, I say:
"Long live the ghosts."

Jacques Derrida

(6) Jacques Derrida. *Ghost Dance.* Directed by Ken McMullen. 1983.

(10) Joseph LeDoux, "How Much of Your Memory Is True?" *Discovery Magazine*, August 3, 2009, http://discovermagazine.com/2009/jul-aug/03-how-much-of-your-memory-is-true

(20) Dean Koontz, *Velocity: A Novel* (New York City, New York: Bantam Publishing, 2005).

(35) David Appelbaum, *Jacques Derrida's Ghost: A Conjuration* (Albany, New York: State University of New York Press, 2009).

(36) Paul Antze and Michael Lambek (Editors), *Tense Past: Cultural Essays in Trauma and Memory* (London: Routledge, 1996).

(37) Arkadii Dragomoshchenko, Trans. Shushan Avagyan, Evgeny Pavlov, Ana Lucic, *Dust* (Champaign, Illinois: Dalkey Archive Press, 2009).

(41) W.G. Sebald, *Campo Santo* (New York City, New York: Modern Library, 2006).

(42) Elaine Scarry, *Dreaming by the Book* (Princeton, New Jersey: Princeton University Press, 2001).

(47) Marilynne Robinson, *Housekeeping: A Novel* (New York City, New York: Farrar, Straus and Giroux, 1980).

(47) Janet Carsten, *Ghosts of Memory: Essays on Remembrance and Relatedness* (Hoboken, New Jersey: Wiley-Blackwell, 2007).

(61) Roland Barthes, *Mourning Diary* (New York City, New York: Hill & Wang, 2010).

(63) Jacques Derrida, "Jacques Derrida and Deconstruction" trans. Mitchell Stephens, dated January 23, 1994, https://www.nyu.edu/classes/stephens/Jacques Derrida - NYT - page.htm

(67) Floyd Skloot, *In the Shadow of Memory* (Lincoln, Nebraska: Bison Books, 2004).

An excerpted selection of a previous version of this essay was selected by John D'Agata as the Grand Prize Winner of the 2011 Black Warrior Review Nonfiction Contest and published as "Fragments from Reconsolidation" in the March 2012 issue of *Black Warrior Review*.

This text was originally composed during 2010-2011, during the period immediately following my mother's death. I'd like to thank the following people for their support in the writing of this text, but also their emotional support in the several years between then and today:

Laura Vena, Joe Milazzo, Jeffrey Uyeno, Anna Joy Springer, Will Alexander, Sueyeun Juliette Lee, Saehee Cho, Shoshana Seidman, Harold Abramowitz, Leon Baham, Eugene Lee, Sal Verduzco, Benny & Maggie.

And so much gratitude for Rebekah Weikel and Penny-Ante Editions.

Janice Lee (2015)

Janice Lee is the author of *Kerotakis* (Dog Horn Press, 2010), *Daughter* (Jaded Ibis, 2011), *Damnation* (Penny-Ante Editions, 2013), and *The Sky Isn't Blue* (Civil Coping Mechanisms, forthcoming 2016). She currently lives in Los Angeles where she is Editor of the #RECURRENT Novel Series for Jaded Ibis Press, Assistant Editor at *Fanzine*, Executive Editor at *Entropy*, and Founder/CEO of POTG Design. She can be found online at janicel.com.

Penny-Ante Editions
PO Box 691578 Los Angeles, California 90069
United States of America
penny-ante.net

Success and Failure Series
Catalogue No. PA-021
ISBN 978-0-9785564-5-7

© Janice Lee, 2015

Printed in the United Sates of America

Book design by Andrea Evangelista
Text set in Lyon and Plakat Narrow
Cover Image: *Joung min Lee*
Courtesy of Janice Lee and Kyung il Lee